CW01664333

THE NEW ADVENTURES OF

ALICE IN RAINFOREST LAND

First published in Australia by Watermark Press / P.I.C
72-80 Cooper St., Surry Hills NSW 2010 Australia
A PIC VENTURE
Text © Nadine Amadio 1988
Illustrations © Charles Blackman 1988

National Library of Australia
cataloguing-in-publication data:

Amadio, Nadine
Alice in rainforest land

ISBN 0 949284 07 6

I. Blackman, Charles, 1928-
II. Title.

A823'.3
Typeset by Solo Typesetting, Adelaide
Design by Nicholson Art Direction

This book is sold subject to the condition that it shall not, by way of trade or otherwise, be lent, resold, hired-out, or otherwise circulated without the publisher's prior consent in any form of binding or cover other than that which it is published and without a similar condition including this condition being imposed on the subsequent purchaser.

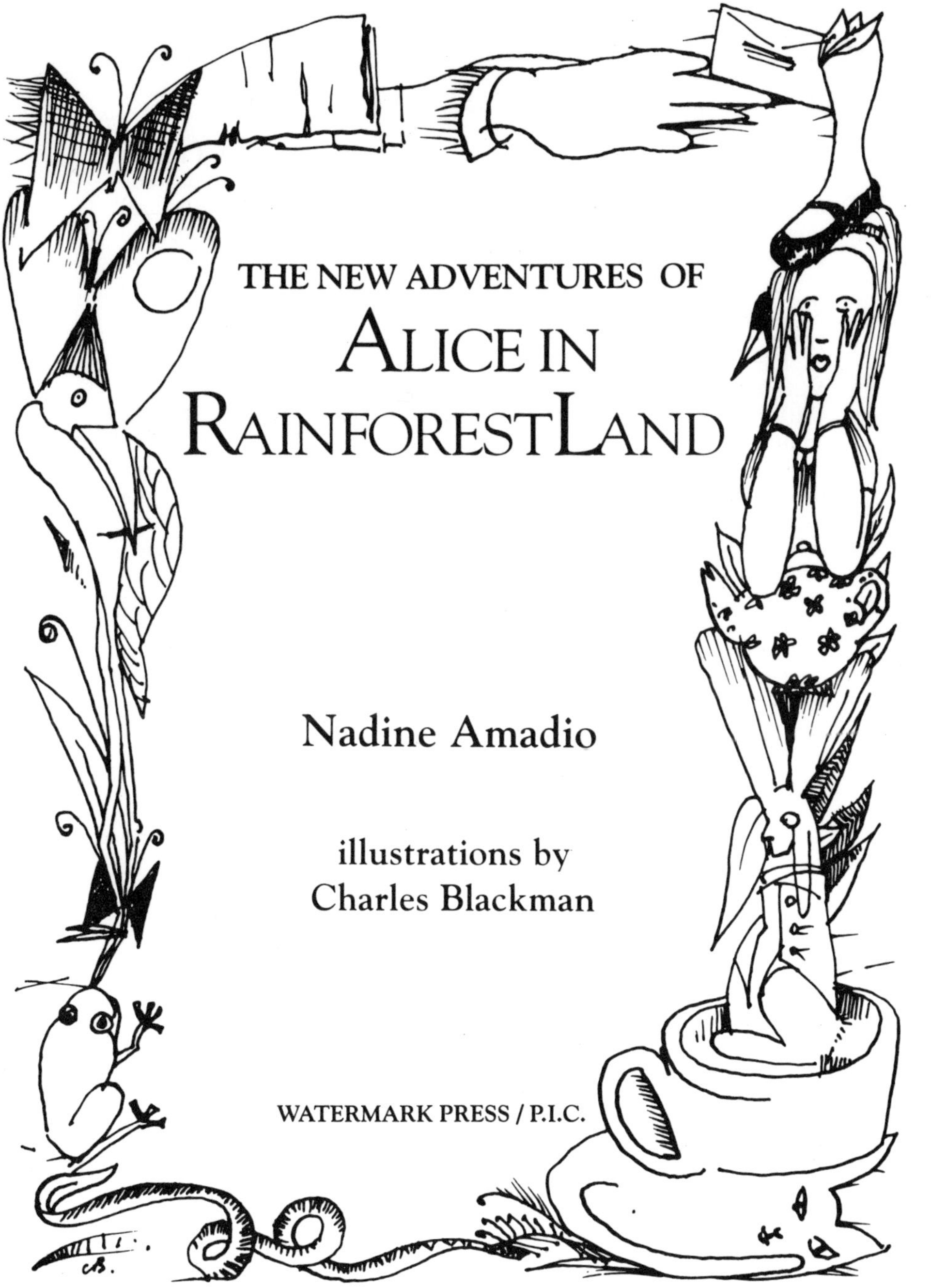

THE NEW ADVENTURES OF

ALICE IN RAINFORESTLAND

Nadine Amadio

illustrations by
Charles Blackman

WATERMARK PRESS / P.I.C.

ACKNOWLEDGEMENTS

First I want to pay homage to that master magician Charles Dodgson who was known to all children as Lewis Carroll, the original creator of Wonderland and of Alice. The spells and images created by the great sorcerers of the past keep working in the world.

However, no-one could write a book about any kind of Wonderland if there weren't magicians alive and well and busy today weaving their magic.

For this reason I would like to thank James Murdoch, Barry Moreland, Brian Howard, Halifax Hayes, Bill Reed, Barrett Reid, Clifford Hocking, John Coburn, John Tristram, Robert Walker, Jonah Jones, and Gabrielle Sunday.

I would also like to pay my own tribute to another master magician, the artist Charles Blackman. Once, an enchanted time ago, he resummoned Alice from her pages in his legendary collection of 'Alice' paintings and made her a great and historic image in art. More recently, and with the same sorcery, he created his inspiring vision of the Australian Rainforest in his 'Rainforest' series of paintings now in the Christensen Fund Collection.

I would also like to thank, for their charming ways, all little girls called Alice or Possie or Madelaine or Beatrice or Marie-Annick, Josefa, Clementine, or some other special name like ...

Finally, I want to thank the Little Friends of the Rainforest. And tree friends everywhere. This book is for them.

Nadine Amadio

CONTENTS

FALLING INTO GREEN

Once upon a time when fields were green and afternoons were golden, Alice sat dreaming and remembering her adventures in Wonderland. She wished she could have another really extraordinary adventure before she grew up. Secretly she knew she would never really grow old but would always stay Alice inside, ready for wonder, but she thought it was really time to open a new door or fall into a new rabbit hole.

She looked at the White Rabbit sunning himself beside her. He had become her best friend and they talked every day about all sorts of interesting things. Not far off, the Cheshire Cat was curled up, fast asleep. He still disappeared regularly but he had come to live with Alice and her other cat, Dinah.

He was, however, still very wild and instead of purring nicely and washing his paws every day, he took great delight in teasing and insulting the White Rabbit. The White Rabbit, who was proud of his manners and, besides, could never think of a really devastating insult at the right moment, chose to ignore the Cheshire Cat and treat him with contempt.

'Do you remember,' said Alice to the White Rabbit, 'when I fell down the rabbit hole into Wonderland?'

The White Rabbit smiled and remembered, and felt in his pocket for his white gloves. They always reminded him of that time.

'Well,' continued Alice, 'I have found another much longer rabbit hole that takes you right through to the other side of the world.'

'Where to?' the White Rabbit asked suspiciously.

'To Australia!' said Alice triumphantly. 'It comes out in a very special sort of Wonderland at the top of Australia called Rainforest Land.

'It's a strange land. It is all green. The sky is green, the air is green. All the trees are green, of course. The snakes and lizards and birds are all green.' Alice knew she was telling a white lie because some of the animals were all sorts of other quite brilliant colours, but it did have a very green feel about it.

'There are cats with six eyes, birds with spoons in their mouths, suitcases with legs that could bite you and snakes so big they could swallow you in one gulp!'

'Indeed!' said the White Rabbit hiding a yawn very politely.

'Yes. We're going today.'

'I'm very busy today,' said the White Rabbit, twitching his whiskers. 'I have to see the Red Queen.'

'Do put off your appointment. I'd be so pleased if you came with me,' Alice said very sweetly. She knew he didn't really have to see the Red Queen at all.

The White Rabbit could hardly refuse such a

charming invitation so he gave his fur a quick brush and they set off to find the very long rabbit hole. When they did they took a deep breath and jumped in.

'It's a long way down, isn't it?' Alice called, making polite conversation, as she toppled and twisted and kept falling for ages until she finally fell right into Australia and the Rainforest.

'Are we there yet?' asked the White Rabbit in a thirsty kind of voice. It had been hours since breakfast. He landed with a thump in a spiky cushion of fronds. Everywhere, as far as the eye could see, were green ferns and leaves. They towered overhead and closed in from all sides. A misty green light enveloped him.

He looked up. Alice was watching him from behind a frond. She had a mysterious look on her face and when she looked like that, he knew in his bones that something very strange was going to happen.

'Hurry up,' said Alice. 'I've been here for hours.'

'That's because you're good at falling and because you knew the way,' said the White Rabbit in a grumpy voice. 'And I'm not going anywhere until I have a cup of tea.'

At that, a huge, brightly coloured Cup and Teapot Butterfly came burbling and splashing along and poured a large cup of tea all over his head.

'Dear, oh dear!' The White Rabbit sat dejectedly, his long furry ears drooping, making hopeless dabbing motions with his handkerchief and muttering to himself.

Alice sympathised and mopped up the White Rabbit. 'There, there!' she exclaimed cheerfully. 'Don't worry too much about being wet. It's wet all the time here. That's why it's called a rainforest. But we are going to have a special tea party and I will show you my butterfly book.'

'Did you say a tea party?' the White Rabbit asked. 'Sparkle, sparkle, little cup,' he quoted, his spirits rising.

'Star! Little star, you mean,' Alice corrected him, politely but firmly.

'No, I mean cup. A sparkling cup of tea.' The White Rabbit did not take kindly to being corrected.

In a soft green clearing in the forest a small table was set with a steaming pot of tea.

A Booyong Tree spread a canopy of leaves and a gauzy curtain of ferns made a forest tea room. A Flame Tree lit the room with tiny scarlet fires.

A comfortable stool was arranged in front of the table and the Cheshire Cat had appeared from nowhere as usual and had settled down under the table with a contented domestic sigh to talk to a small marsupial.

A swarm of local butterflies eager for news about their exotic imaginary relations gathered around for the grand opening of the book.

The White Rabbit was quite restored to his usual good humour and squeezed up beside Alice on the stool, brushed his whiskers up and sipped at his tea. They opened the large butterfly book on their knees.

'I know all about butterflies,' Alice said modestly. 'Did you know, for instance, that a book of butterflies is far superior to a book of stamps?'

'Indeed,' said the Rabbit, sounding surprised.

'For with stamps, the pictures stay in the book, but, with butterflies, you open the book and they immediately fly out and around the room. When you close it,' she said, decisively, 'they all return to their places.' She snapped the book shut.

'Or, one hopes they will,' she added, with not the same degree of conviction as she saw a butterfly that glistened like a pool of tears fluttering by.

'How interesting,' murmured the White Rabbit.

'Look out!' called Alice.

But it was too late. The curious Pool of Tears Butterfly had come to have a closer look at the White Rabbit and had wept copiously all over him.

'Now I'm drenched again!' the White Rabbit grumbled. His damp ears drooped with dismay and the ends of his whiskers had tiny diamond tears on them.

Alice, whose manners were impeccable, turned her head so he wouldn't see her laughing.

The Cheshire Cat, who was quite dry and, as we all know, was sadly lacking in good manners, made no secret about smiling quite smugly at the dripping rabbit.

Once again, Alice mopped him and cheered him up. The White Rabbit was getting distinctly grumpy.

Suddenly, there was a strange noise in the forest.

'What's that?' the White Rabbit asked nervously.

'Oh, just a Pouched Frog,' Alice said nonchalantly.

'Or maybe a Long-nosed Potoroo,' she added.

The noise grew louder and more unusual and Alice's shoes jumped right off her feet without even undoing their buttons, gave themselves a quick polish and flew off into the evening to see what the noise was all about. 'Come back at once,' cried Alice with annoyance, but they took no notice at all.

Alice and the White Rabbit proceeded on foot into the gloom of the forest to investigate the noise.

They travelled slowly because Alice kept getting stones and prickles in her feet. 'I do hope my shoes come home soon,' she said wistfully. 'They developed this habit of wandering off ever since someone addressed a letter to them in Wonderland. It quite went to their feet.'

As they drew closer to the source they could hear a mournful moaning sound as if someone were in great pain. It was actually someone singing, but terribly out of tune.

'I think it is a wounded wombat or a crocodile with toothache,' said the Cheshire Cat scornfully.

'Whatever it is, it's perfectly dreadful and decidedly unmusical,' Alice snapped. 'I can't bear it. Let's go.'

'Oh no you don't,' said a chilling, groaning voice. 'I want you to Wait Awhile. I want to sing you my song. I'm a Wait Awhile Vine and I'm a singer.'

'I'm afraid I will have to correct you,' said Alice somewhat tartly. 'You might well be a vine but you are certainly not a singer.'

They turned to go and found that the Wait Awhile Vine had wrapped hundreds of little claws around them. They desperately tried to prise them off but more would clasp them in a sharp embrace. They feared they would be there for ever and looked frantically round for help.

'Wait Awhile and hear my song,' moaned the relentless vine.

'I don't want to wait awhile,' cried the White Rabbit, tearing at the sharp claws in panic. 'I would rather walk on.'

'Good idea! There's a lot to be said for walking. I have a brisk walk every day after lunch without fail,' said a firm military voice. A Walking-stick Palm, fronds alert, strode into view.

'You're in a spot of trouble, aren't you?' he asked the White Rabbit. 'That's what comes of associating with vines,' he said scornfully. 'They never walk anywhere. They just creep!'

The Walking-stick Palm slapped the Wait Awhile sharply across the knuckles. 'Let go! You impudent Vine. Let go immediately.'

The Wait Awhile gave a cry of frustration and was forced to let go. He slunk back into the green gloom and the Walking-stick Palm marched on.

'Oh thank you, Mr Palm,' Alice called after him.

'Think nothing of it.' The Palm stopped and saluted them and then strode off again.

Alice collapsed on the forest floor. 'What an alarming creature that Wait Awhile Vine is,' she gasped. 'We must keep well away from him in future.'

'I don't know what was worse,' grumbled the White Rabbit, 'his claws or his singing.'

Just then Alice's shoes flew by. She jumped up and caught them and buttoned them up tightly.

'Please do not fly away again,' she said severely.

'I can't walk through the forest barefoot. Next time I'll wear my gum-boots.'

Suitably ashamed, her shoes settled down, wrapped around her feet, and became very docile and shoelike. They promised to devote themselves entirely to her feet in future and protect her always.

Alice and the White Rabbit, having first removed themselves from the vicinity of the Wait Awhile Vine, settled down to have a little rest.

They looked around in wonder at the huge trees and the ferns. The trees seemed to tower up almost out of sight. 'You know, this rainforest took four hundred million years to grow,' said Alice.

The White Rabbit lifted a weary head. 'That's a long, long time,' he said sleepily. 'It makes me very tired to even imagine it.'

'It makes it very precious,' said Alice softly. 'Probably the most precious thing in the world!'

THE SONG OF CHANGING

When they had rested for a while, and quite recovered from their unpleasant encounter with the Wait Awhile Vine, Alice, the White Rabbit and the Cheshire Cat set out to explore the forest.

The birds and creatures of the forest nodded to them in quite a friendly way as they passed along.

Alice always took care to say 'Good morning' very politely to everyone even if they didn't answer. You never knew where strange or maybe even dangerous creatures were hiding in the forest.

They had not gone far before they saw a webbed twiggy sort of thing hanging from a tree.

'What's that?' asked the White Rabbit.

'That's a chrysalis,' said Alice; 'and I'm glad you asked me about it because it's very special.

'I've been thinking about the way things change,' she said. 'Most things in the forest change and grow but none of them change so wonderfully as the funny little caterpillar that lives in that stick house. I'll sing you the song about it.'

And as they walked deeper into the forest Alice sang them "The Song of Changing".

THE SONG OF CHANGING

There's a long long word that could make you sing:
Metamorphosis is its name.
When a thing turns into a quite different thing,
It's like a magical game.

Take a crinkly stick that's a stickily house,
Called a chrysalis, full of old worm.
Then it stirs and changes and wants to leave home;
It's a case of the worm that turns.

The very plain caterpillar—for that's all it was—
Calls out with a great joyous cry
As it bursts from its bed you can see it has changed
To a breathtaking butterfly!

So creepy old crawlies can grow, as you see,
Into shining new beauties with wings;
And magic and change are around all the time,
And things can become other things.

'You mean the White Rabbit might change into something beautiful one day?' the Cheshire Cat asked innocently.

No one got irritated or took any notice of the Cheshire Cat, rather to his annoyance, because it was such a perfect day and the notion of things changing was fascinating and took a lot of thinking about.

Suddenly, there was a gentle flapping sound and a huge, brightly coloured butterfly perched beside them on a branch. 'I was listening to your song,' it said in a sweet, fluting voice, 'and I liked it very much. It sounded as if you liked butterflies.'

'Oh, I do,' cried Alice. 'You are my favourite creatures of the forest. You are very beautiful,' she added shyly.

The butterfly, who looked as if it were made of flowers, held its wings up to the light. 'Yes, I suppose I am,' she sighed. 'We butterflies live and fly high up in the canopies of the forest. We are the stained-glass windows of the great Forest Cathedral.'

'That sounds wonderful,' breathed Alice.

'Would you like to really be part of the Rainforest? Would you like to come and see?' asked the Floral Butterfly. 'Just come closer and look into the window.'

The butterfly grew bigger and bigger and Alice and the White Rabbit came up close and looked through the great coloured windows of its wings. Inside was a high and airy butterfly garden where thousands of bright-winged butterflies fluttered and flew.

They were enchanted with the view into this world and longed to visit there.

'Just step through the window,' whispered the butterfly. So they stood on their tiptoes and stepped right in.

Suddenly, the White Rabbit had the most curious sensation. He felt himself getting flatter and lighter and dividing into two halves.

'Oh dear! Oh dear!' cried the White Rabbit. 'I think I'm meta—metamorph—I think I'm changing

into a butterfly! What am I going to do? I don't know if I'm going to like being a butterfly. I'd got rather used to being a rabbit.'

'Well, at least you'll have wings,' Alice said, consolingly.

'Yes. I suppose that's true,' said the White Rabbit rather grudgingly. He waited until his long ears had changed into wings and then he launched himself into the melting green vault of the Rainforest and floated off on his first flight.

'Wheeee. Look at me! I'm flying.' The White Rabbit's tiny silky scream reached Alice and she waved encouragingly.

'Come on!' he called. 'Come and fly. It's wonderful!' And he flapped his radiant earwings and dived and circled right under Alice's nose.

Alice threw up her arms and leaped up like a dancer or a dolphin and in one magical movement she became Alice Butterfly and joined the White Rabbit on his joy-flight of the forest.

They swooped and flapped through the high branches and with their butterfly's-eye view saw the ancient wonder of the Rainforest; its green banners flying, its delicate patterns forever changing with the light.

'Come on now, let's have a real fly together,' Alice called to the White Rabbit. They took off joyously, sometimes dancing around each other, almost becoming one giant butterfly.

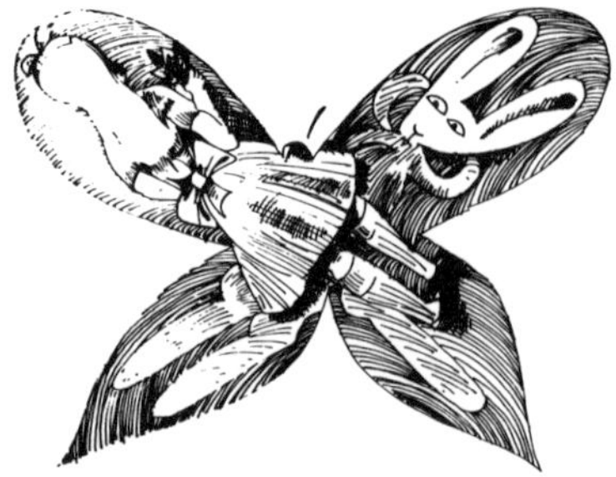

They flew through the hundreds of different trees, up, up, into the great airy gardens that grow among the high canopy of trees.

Rays of light lit their wings. They felt radiant and happy, they knew what it was like to become the stained-glass windows in this great living cathedral.

They rested on the giant elkhorns, they peered into birds' nests. They swam down into the gloom where a thousand vines, ferns, orchids and mosses festooned the huge buttressed trees.

Brilliant Wheels of Fire spun as they flew by and everywhere little hidden shining eyes watched them in their flight of celebration.

After they had flown round for a whole long day they became tired. They weren't quite sure what butterflies did at night and where they slept.

'We must become ourselves again now,' said Alice when their long flight was over. 'It was wonderful, but it's quite exhausting being a butterfly.'

'Yes, it is and I'm tired, too. But how?' inquired the White Rabbit.

'We'll have to find the Floral Butterfly,' said Alice.

'That mightn't be very easy,' muttered the Rabbit darkly. His ears were aching from all that flapping.

'Excuse me, sir,' said Alice, addressing a handsome green and gold Cairns Birdwing Butterfly, who was idly munching a small bunch of berries. 'Have you seen the Floral Butterfly anywhere?'

'Yes, I think I could tell you,' he mused. 'Do you have a pencil to write down the address?'

'No, I don't,' Alice answered rather indignantly. 'You can see I'm a butterfly and I don't have hands, or a pencil for that matter.'

'How inconvenient for you,' he murmured.

'Well, you don't either,' said Alice.

'How do you know what I have or don't have? You are a most presumptuous young lady,' drawled the Birdwing Butterfly.

Alice was about to fly off in a huff when she realised she could be hours trying to find the Floral Butterfly.

'I am very sorry if I've been rude,' she said politely. 'If you tell me clearly, I might be able to memorise the address.'

'Well,' said the Birdwing, somewhat mollified, 'I think you might find her on the topmost branch of this very tree. You'll find,' he added languidly, 'they are admiring my wife's fine new spring wardrobe. They say she'll look just like me.' He shrugged his splendid wings modestly.

Alice contained her irritation and with the White Rabbit reached the top of the very high tree, and there was the Floral Butterfly large and shining in the late sun.

'My poor dears,' she said in a comforting voice. 'You look very tired.'

'We are,' said Alice. 'Could we please fly through your window and change again?'

'Yes. But you must wait until we fly down to the

ground. If you came through the window here you would topple all the way down without wings.'

So they flew down to the forest floor and the Floral Butterfly opened her winged windows again and Alice Butterfly and the White Rabbit Butterfly flew through and immediately became themselves again.

They felt huge and extremely heavy and there were no wings any more, only sharp shoulder blades. They felt a deep sense of loss.

'Did you enjoy your day of being butterflies?' asked the Floral Butterfly, as she prepared to depart.

She looked round to see why they didn't answer. She smiled when she saw them. They were both propped up against a tree fast asleep.

RAINFOREST DREAMING

'We seem to be very small,' said Alice, stretching and yawning after a long, refreshing sleep. She looked at the White Rabbit and around at the towering ferns. 'I have the distinct feeling that the Floral Butterfly forgot our original size. Now we are so small we might be in danger,' she said a bit tearfully to the White Rabbit, who started nervously twisting his gloves.

He produced his opera glasses and peered at Alice. 'My word, you are very small,' he said in dismay. 'I could look at you through my telescope,' he offered gallantly. 'Maybe that would help.'

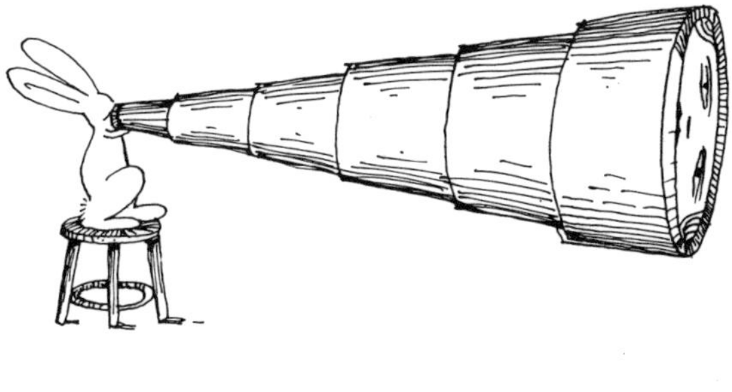

'Don't worry. I can help you,' called a cheerful velvety voice that sounded like the softest koala. Imagine their surprise when a huge fellow came lumbering through the forest with large spikes sticking out of his back.

'Goodness me!' Alice said, with a shaky voice. 'Who are you?'

'I am Echidna,' the spiked creature announced. 'I'm a fairly well-known poet,' he added modestly, raising his rich velvety voice and pointing his long nose in the air.

'I'm sure you must be quite famous with your beautiful way of speaking,' Alice said, deciding polite conversation was perhaps the wisest way to deal with large spiked creatures, and wondering if she were not being lulled into a false sense of security by his winsome voice.

'Yes. I suppose I am quite famous,' the Echidna admitted graciously and sighed. 'I have been watching you for a long time, you know. I thought you all looked so strange and interesting, I might write a poem about you.'

'What a perfectly charming idea,' Alice smiled.

The Echidna's sharp little eyes glittered with pleasure. 'The last poem I wrote was about my cousin the Platypus. He's very odd and quite a celebrity.'

'Yes,' said Alice breathlessly. 'I know all about the Australian Platypus. They taught us at school how extraordinary it is and how it has a bill like a duck and webbed feet and a furry body, and—'. She stopped, seeing the Echidna's disappointed face. 'But, I'd love to hear your poem—some time.'

'But first I'll take you to a special berry bush I know,' said Echidna, cheerful again. 'They have the strangest gingery taste and if you eat them, they make you grow. So climb up on my back and I'll take you there.'

'You are very kind,' murmured Alice, who was growing quite fond of this spiky fellow with the mellow voice.

Echidna lowered himself, which really didn't make much difference as his legs were tiny and he was almost round. Alice and the White Rabbit scrambled up on his back and he rose to his feet and lumbered off.

Alice stood up, swaying and holding on to a spike as she rode, the wind blowing through her hair. As the Echidna crashed and thundered through the forest, she thought to herself how much the Queen of Hearts would have loved to travel like this in a huge spiked chariot.

And while they swayed and clumped along, the Echidna made lovely warm rumbling humming noises that had the same comforting feeling as warm toast cooking in the kitchen, or rain on the roof.

Suddenly, the Echidna ground to a halt in front of a small possum who was waving his paws frantically for the Echidna to stop.

'Well, what is all this waving about?' inquired the Echidna. 'Move along now, you're blocking my way.'

'Someone very important wants to see them,' whispered the Possum mysteriously, pointing his thumb several times at Alice and the White Rabbit.

'I do wish you would speak up,' said the Echidna in a ringing voice. 'Who wants to see them?'

The Possum looked around to see who might be

listening and then, patting his shiny coat, he drew himself up and announced in a theatrical voice, 'The Guardian wants to see them.'

The Echidna gasped. 'The Guardian?'

'Yes,' said the Possum, delighted with the effect he was having. 'And,' he paused, looked at them sternly and added darkly, 'as soon as possible!'

'Yes. Yes. Of course. Of course. Yes. Yes. Right away. Right away,' the Echidna agreed, repeating himself, Alice thought, in the silliest kind of way.

'Wait a minute!' said Alice, sliding off the Echidna's back and coming round the front to face him. 'I thought we were going to find the berries. I don't want to see some old guardian.'

'We have no choice,' said the Echidna gravely.

'He only talks every thousand years or so. He is very old and very wise. He is the one who holds the vision of the Rainforest's Dream and no one in the forest would ever even think of disobeying him. Goodness knows what would happen if we did. I dread to think,' the Echidna said, shivering.

'Is he a sort of a King? Fierce like the Queen of Hearts? An "off with your head" sort of King?' Alice asked uneasily.

'No. Nothing like that.' The Echidna shook his head slowly. 'He is our Guardian. He understands all our patterns. All our dreams and our essences. It's hard even for a poet to explain the Guardian,' and his head drooped sadly.

'Of course, we must go then,' said Alice promptly, anxious to cheer up the Echidna and very curious by now.

So Alice clambered up on his back again and they set off to the place of the Guardian. It was a long way and they moved slowly. The Echidna was trying not to crash about too much now that he had a royal command. However, he often forgot to be solemn and would start his rumbling, humming sound so his whole body vibrated as he sang sweetly to himself.

They finally came to a small clearing and the Echidna looked around in dismay. He couldn't tell where to go from here. There seemed to be a wall of vines and ferns all around. They were trapped.

Two large yellow eyes blinked open on the tree in front of them and a large owl-like bird, a Tawny Frogmouth, hooted at them imperiously.

The Frogmouth with its stony feathers and cold manner seemed built into the tree like a medieval gargoyle.

'Where do you think you are going? Kindly leave immediately,' it demanded. Then, leaning forward so it nearly toppled off the tree, the Frogmouth asked in sinister hooting tones, 'Do you want to disturb the Guardian?'

'No. Not at all. I wouldn't dream of it. That is to say, yes. Yes I do.' The Echidna was flustered.

'Tell him we were summoned,' hissed Alice, leaning down to where she thought his ear should be.

The Echidna nodded gratefully. He straightened his spikes. 'The Guardian has summoned us,' he said grandly. 'You must please tell us the way.'

The Frogmouth looked a bit disbelieving and ruffled his feathers as if he were arguing with himself. But finally he agreed to let them pass and pointed the way, reciting in a hooting sing-song voice.

THE WAY THROUGH THE FOREST

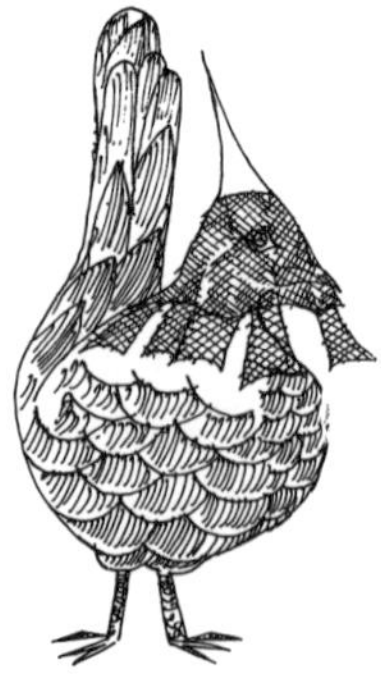

You take the turn to the right past the
Cheesecake Tree,
While singing a Sassafras song.
Blow on three dandelions very hard,
And skip past the Black Booyong.

You take the turn to the left past the
Tuckeroo Tree,
And see if there's anyone there.
Ask the Purple-crowned Pigeon in the
Lace Flower Tree,
'Which way next?' But mind you don't stare!

You hop three times round the
Kurrajong Tree,
Then walk backwards until you forget.
You count all the leaves on the
Bloodwood Tree
And see if you've got there yet.

The Frogmouth paused and the Echidna looked over his shoulder at Alice as best he could, and said in a worried voice, 'I hope you are taking a note of all this.'

'Oh, how can I?' Alice asked. 'Those sort of directions would just drive you crazy! They don't make sense.'

'Not to people who are crazy already!' said the Frogmouth rather acidly. 'Sane people like us find them quite explicit and, anyway, as you find or don't find your way, you have a lesson in botany besides.'

'Say it again, Frogmouth,' demanded the Echidna, who couldn't remember any of the directions at all, even though he was a poet.

But a stony silence had overtaken the Frogmouth

and his yellow eyes were firmly closed.

Just then, the same Possum who had brought their summons came rushing up. 'Haven't you got there yet?' he said with irritation. 'I delivered the message hours ago.'

'We don't know the way,' Alice called.

'Well, follow me,' said the Possum and he skipped off through the forest with the Echidna hurrying behind, swaying like an overloaded double-decker bus.

At last, the Possum slowed down and pointed in front of him. 'In there,' he said.

Alice and the White Rabbit slid off the Echidna's back and the three of them stepped into a large clearing.

There was a large Rainforest Pool, so still and dark it was almost black. The pool was surrounded by lacy feathery ferns but nothing grew or moved on the surface. It was as if the water was sleeping.

And straight in front was the biggest tree Alice had ever seen. A giant of a tree, whose buttressed roots ran deep down into the dark pool.

The three of them stood awed and wondering what to do next. Alice gathered up her courage and, much to the surprise of the others, she addressed the great tree.

'Are you the Guardian?' she asked.

The tree sighed and yawned and said in a thrilling voice that gave Alice gooseprickles. 'Yes, I am. And I am very very old.'

'I can see that,' said Alice meekly. 'Would it be rude to ask you what you do?'

'I am the Minder of Dreams,' said the great tree. 'I hold the dreams of everyone and everything. All the creatures in this Rainforest and everyone in the world. As they take in the breath that the forest makes for them, they breathe out their dreams for us to mind. I make each one into a tiny leaf and guard it forever.

'As long as the rainforest lives, men will breathe and dreams will grow.'

'Oh,' said Alice, because she could hardly say anything else.

And then, she asked shyly, 'Do you have my dream?'

'Yes. I have your dream. It is still the bright and tumbling dream of a child. Do you want to see it?'

'Oh! Yes.' Alice breathed with excitement.

'Come to the edge of the pool and keep very still,' sighed the tree.

The three friends came close to the dark pool's edge and stood quietly.

Suddenly, a wind blew up and tossed the branches of the tree. In the pool, the shadows of the leaves knitted and unknitted themselves in shivering movements like swift wild weavers.

Then the shadowy weaving stopped and one silvery leaf was reflected in the heart of the pool. It seemed to spin and send silver lines skimming across the pool, as if it were an artist drawing her dreams.

They all gasped, for there on the surface of the pool were reflected all her adventures, all her wonder, her friends, her childhood. That was her dream.

She looked for a long time, until she burst with delight, and started jumping and laughing, and whirling and laughing, and the dream fractured into tiny jewels and rippled away, and the pool was still again.

The Guardian looked down at her and laughed too, and it was a mighty sound like the most wonderful music. Like the bright music dreams of all the great composers.

As long as she lived Alice would remember the sound of the Guardian laughing. It was the sound of a forest of birds singing, a skyful of stars

sparkling and the sound of dreams shimmering.

Every creature in the forest stopped and listened and, with Alice, waited until the last notes had pealed and echoed away. It was a bright day in the forest.

'You know so much for someone who doesn't travel about,' said Alice.

'I'm too busy to travel much,' said the Guardian. 'Have you ever felt how delicious it is to just stay home and work and think in your own mindhouse? Anyway, you can travel anywhere at all from there if you want to.'

'Why did you show me my dream?' Alice asked quietly.

'There will come a day when we will need friends,' said the Guardian. 'Men will forget that their children need to breathe and dream. You will remember.'

'I will be your friend,' Alice vowed. 'What do you want me to do?' But the Guardian had gone back to work and would talk no more.

She heard a humming noise and at first thought it was the Echidna, but it was the smaller trees on the other side of the pool, and a song hummed and sighed through their branches as they went about their work.

'You will remember,' sighed the leaves at the top of the tree. 'You will remember.'

But Alice was worried: 'I know everyone needs friends,' she said to the smaller trees, 'but nothing could really ever harm you, could it?'

'There are those who chop down trees,' they whispered gravely and the wind through their leaves sighed and shivered.

Alice was sad and bewildered. She could not really believe that anyone would chop down a rain-forest tree. She sat down beside the pool and in her sadness she sang this song to the trees.

ALICE'S SONG

Would they chop down a dream?
Could they ungrow a tree?
Would they fell to the ground
Something standing and free?

Could they unmake the leaves
So the wind never stirred?
Could they unpaint the colours?
Would they send home the birds?

Could they lower those wide arms
With the fingers of green?
Would they dig out their toes?
Would they chop down a dream?

'No! No!, called hundreds of tiny voices. It was the insects and small animals that had stopped to hear Alice's sad song.

'Well, we won't let it happen,' said Alice in her firmest voice and everyone immediately felt more cheerful. But the wind in the trees still sighed 'Remember, remember.'

Alice knew she always would.

TAILS TO TELL

As Alice, the White Rabbit and the Echidna stood by the edge of the pool, still half in a dream after their meeting with the Guardian, they felt a tugging at their arms.

It was the Possum. 'Come on,' he insisted. 'We aren't supposed to stay here by the dark pool. No one can look into the pool for too long.'

'Why?' asked Alice, always curious.

'I think, perhaps, they would go mad,' said the Possum thoughtfully. 'Come on!'

So Alice and the White Rabbit climbed up on the Echidna's back and they slowly made their way out of the clearing.

They were all rather quiet. Meeting the Guardian made you feel like being quiet for a while. They didn't talk about it much and after a while they began to wonder if they had dreamed the whole meeting.

But nothing could dampen the Echidna's spirits for long, and soon they began to hear the jolly rumbling noise that meant the Echidna was humming one of his songs or poems to himself.

After a very long journey, Alice started to see signs of places she remembered and now they were close to the clearing where Alice kept her teapot and cups.

'We seem to have come a full circle,' she called into the Echidna's ear. 'We are almost back to the place where we started.'

'Ah, well,' said the Echidna wisely, 'then we must be close to finding what we are searching for.' And, with that, he started snuffling around under trees and shrubs looking for the berries he had promised to find.

Alice was irritated. 'We've made that long journey all around for nothing,' she grumbled.

'Hardly for nothing,' said the Echidna, looking over his shoulder. 'Besides, we would never have found the berries if we had come straight across them.'

Alice felt he was probably right so she slid off his back and waited while he snuffled around. The White Rabbit, who had been rather quiet during the journey, slid down too.

'Are you all right?' she asked the White Rabbit.

'Well, I was a bit sea-sick,' he admitted. 'I'm used to scampering and even falling down holes, but swaying along doesn't actually agree with me.' And with that he turned a tiny bit green and blended in with the ferns.

The Echidna had wandered off out of sight, so Alice and the White Rabbit decided they'd better wait where they were in case they got lost. They settled down against a tree and prepared to have a little snooze after all their travels.

'Are you frightened? Are you frightened of me?' boomed a raspy voice from above them.

Alice and the White Rabbit clasped each other in

fear and slowly raised their eyes. It was worse than they had possibly imagined.

A gigantic dinosaur straight from the Mesozoic era loomed above them covered in scales. Its back was raised in saw-toothed spikes, and heavy-lidded reptilian eyes fixed them with a beady glitter.

'Heavens!' The White Rabbit shivered. 'What a monster!' He put a protective paw around Alice's shoulder.

The dinosaur seemed quite pleased at the effect he was having. 'I am rather a terrifying monster, aren't I? Are you frightened of me?'

'Yes. Yes. We certainly are,' agreed the White Rabbit immediately, hoping he would leave.

'I'm a Dragon. A Rainforest Dragon,' he announced, with, Alice believed, entirely unjustified pride.

'Do you eat people or rabbits?' Alice asked, gathering her courage.

'Sometimes, if I'm really hungry,' snarled the Dragon, puffing out a large pouch under his neck to make himself more fearsome.

'Oh, dear!' Alice nearly fainted with fright, and tried to creep backwards into the forest.

The Dragon swished his long barbed tail and growled, 'I might eat you up right now, but I'll sing you my song first! Please listen carefully.'

He swivelled his long tail around beside him, because he had actually written his song on his tail in case he forgot it.

THE DRAGON'S TAIL

I'm a dangerous Rainforest Dragon,
As fierce as can possibly be.
I'm a barbaric prehistoric predator—
Don't invite me home to tea.

I'd probably chew up the furniture—
That's after I'd eaten you.
I'd rudely polish my scales on the curtains
And then I'd eat them and the carpet up, too.

I can hold my claws in the creepiest way,
And bare the sharpest fang.
I'd terrorise the neighbourhood
Without the slightest pang.

I'm a ravenous Rainforest Dragon.
I fill you with dread and dislike,
With my great puffed throat and my wicked scales,
And my razor-back armed with its spikes.

By this time he was nearly down to the tip of his tail and Alice and the White Rabbit were nearly down to the last of their courage when a loud, derisive voice interrupted.

'Booo!' called the voice. 'Call that a poem? That's the worst poem I've ever heard!'

They looked up to where a large Noisy Pitta sat preening its feathers on the branch above.

'And as for terrifying little girls and rabbits. That's pathetic. You couldn't eat them if you tried. We're all getting a bit sick of your theatrical behaviour. You're just an old ham!'

The Noisy Pitta leaned forward and said to Alice: 'He's got an extremely inflated idea of himself. Just ignore him.'

'Oh!, I wish I'd known that earlier,' cried Alice, still trembling.

The Dragon looked up in annoyance. 'You're spoiling my fun,' he complained. 'I really had them frightened.'

'Not very,' denied the Rabbit in a shivering voice.

'Not much. I had you half scared to death,' and the vulgar Dragon laughed much too loudly.

Just then the Echidna returned with two beautiful blue ginger berries. He saw the Dragon. 'What's going on here?' he demanded.

'We have been so frightened,' cried Alice.

'What! Of that stupid overgrown lizard?' the Echidna asked with contempt. 'Get away, you thorny-tailed shrimp!'

The Dragon scuttled back into the forest and the Noisy Pitta whistled scornfully after him.

'Here, eat these,' said the Echidna, 'then pompous little dragons won't frighten you any more.'

Alice and the White Rabbit ate the enchanting blue berries and straight away they grew much larger.

They still weren't back to full size but at least they were now the same size as the Echidna and the larger birds. It was a great relief.

'You've been very kind to us,' said Alice to the Echidna. I must have a tea party for you. And for you, too,' she called to the Noisy Pitta, who had remained above to see the end of the adventure.

Just then, there was a terrible shriek in the forest nearby and Alice thought she recognised the not altogether dulcet tones of the Cheshire Cat.

They all rushed into the forest and there, underneath a Tamarind Tree, a large python was trying to swallow the Cheshire Cat.

Alice and the White Rabbit rushed up and, not even stopping to feel afraid, they pulled with all their strength on each tail.

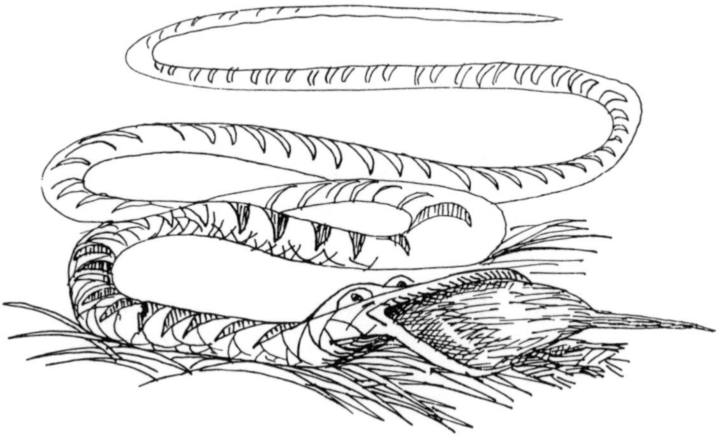

The White Rabbit grabbed the Cheshire Cat's tail and Alice firmly grasped the python's tail. They kept pulling, as if they were playing a desperate game of tug o' war. Suddenly, they heard a terrific plopping sound and out came the Cheshire Cat, and head over heels tumbled Alice and the White Rabbit into a bed of ferns.

The disappointed python wriggled sinuously away into the forest.

The Cheshire Cat felt most humiliated at his rescue and far from being grateful was most upset. What followed was really rather disgraceful and very ill-mannered.

The Cheshire Cat bowed stiffly to Alice and then swept right by the White Rabbit without even nodding in his direction. The White Rabbit, who had quite exhausted himself in his cat-saving effort, was extremely annoyed, to say the least.

He made a few taunting remarks to the Cheshire Cat, who responded, one is obliged to say, with several quite unspeakable insults.

What followed was a fight almost too terrible to behold. Alice was very upset and walked away in disgust.

However, the Echidna stayed and watched until

the bitter end. He flattered himself that he was quite a connoisseur of fights and often, if he were feeling inspired, would turn them into heroic couplets. He rather thought this particular fight might lend itself to a minor epic poem.

Alice stayed away from the fight until things calmed down, thus missing several historic insults. Then she returned, at which stage she forced them to embrace and make up, which they did very grudgingly indeed.

Alice turned on her heel and walked off. 'And don't let it happen again. I am ashamed of you,' she snapped.

Alice was preparing for her tea party when she heard a loud 'Harumph', like someone clearing his throat. She turned to see the Rainforest Dragon looking very dejected, standing in front of her.

'I've come to apologise,' he stammered. 'The birds have been giving me a hard time because I was so rude and unpleasant. I didn't really mean it. It was all a joke, you know. No one is at all scared of me.'

Alice looked at the Dragon, who was hardly frightening at all now she had grown larger. 'You were quite terrible,' she reflected.

'Yes. Yes, I was,' the Dragon agreed eagerly.

'I suppose I should forgive you,' Alice considered. 'After all, I used to know someone far worse than you. This someone used to scream: "Off with his head!" to almost everyone she ever met.'

'Oh, that's dreadful!' exclaimed the Dragon, with

a hint of self-righteous indignation. 'I could never do anything quite as beastly as that.'

'Well, all right then,' said Alice, who prided herself on her forgiving nature. She held out a hand rather cautiously.

The Dragon shook hands very gently, anxious now to create a good impression.

'I hear,' said the Dragon, very casually, 'that you are giving a tea party. Do you think I might come?'

'But you distinctly said in your song that no one should ever invite you to tea.'

'That's only because I always hope someone will,' said the Dragon, rather wistfully.

'Well, you can come after the speeches and poems.' Alice felt it would have been mean to refuse.

'Are there going to be speeches and poems?'

'So I've been led to believe,' Alice said.

'Well, could I come halfway through the party? Then I would only be half there and not nearly so upsetting to anyone.'

By this time Alice had quite forgiven the silly Dragon, so she agreed and he went off, swishing his spiky tail in delight.

THE POET'S TEA PARTY

After their exhausting adventures they all needed a nice comforting tea party to restore their spirits. Alice wrote neat little cards saying, 'Echidna' and 'Noisy Pitta' and 'White Rabbit' and then, after some deliberation, she added 'Dragon'; and she laid the table with a snowy white cloth, clean napkins in their rings and a cup and plate for everyone. There was a large pot of steaming tea and an absolutely scrumptious chocolate cake.

Above them hung the fronds of several giant elkhorns and vines, and ferns crowded in on them everywhere. A collection of beetles and caterpillars, who hadn't been invited, waited under the table—at the opposite end to the Cheshire Cat—in case some delicious crumbs should fall.

The Echidna and the Noisy Pitta arrived early, looking very neat and clean, and hurried to sit down. They pulled up their chairs made of woven leaves.

They all tucked their napkins under their chins and for a long time they ate and sipped in silence and sheer contentment, bathed in a soft green light.

Then, the Noisy Pitta fell to musing. He was well aware of his remarkable turquoise and gold feathered beauty and his loud, strong voice. He privately thought he would have made a fine opera singer. A handsome feathered fellow such as he could bring nothing but acclaim to any opera company. A role such as Papageno in *The Magic Flute* would have suited him admirably.

Alice was indeed fortunate he had accepted her invitation to tea. He knew he was an admirable guest. Polite and attractive and something of a conversationalist. Even the flowers listened when he spoke.

He puffed out his feathers and moved to the end of the table so he could turn his good profile to the company.

The conversation turned to that creeping, crawling, obnoxious pest with the razor-sharp claws, the Lawyer Vine or the Wait Awhile Vine. Alice shivered as she remembered their encounter with this forest monster and looked around anxiously to make sure there were none in the vicinity.

But the Noisy Pitta had deliberately directed the conversation to the Wait Awhile Vine because he had written a song about it and he could hardly wait to sing it to everyone.

He suddenly stood up, untied his napkin and placed it beside him neatly and coughed discreetly. They all turned to see why he was coughing, so he made his announcement.

'I saw your whole adventure,' said the Noisy Pitta. 'Allow me to refresh your memory. I have made it into a song.'

No one could stop him. Besides, it was rather nice being made into a forest legend and having people sing about you, Alice and the White Rabbit thought.

So the Noisy Pitta cleared his throat, did a few scales to warm up, noticing with pleasure how his voice cascaded in liquid notes and trills, and then he began.

To be quite honest, it was not really much of a melody, Alice privately thought. It went up and down a lot, like the scales she had to practise for her piano teacher, but the words were quite interesting and the Noisy Pitta did sing quite charmingly.

THE SONG OF THE WAIT AWHILE VINE

Alice, the Rabbit and an erstwhile toad
Plunged into the rainforest's dream.
Their teeth were brushed, their intentions pure,
And their hair had a healthy gleam.
What happened to them on this fateful day?
Careful! Things are not quite what they seem.

A secret singer, a sighing vine,
Whose motives were sadly wrong,
Planned to make travellers Wait Awhile
To hear its uninteresting song.
We all know such boring characters—
And their wind is by far too long.

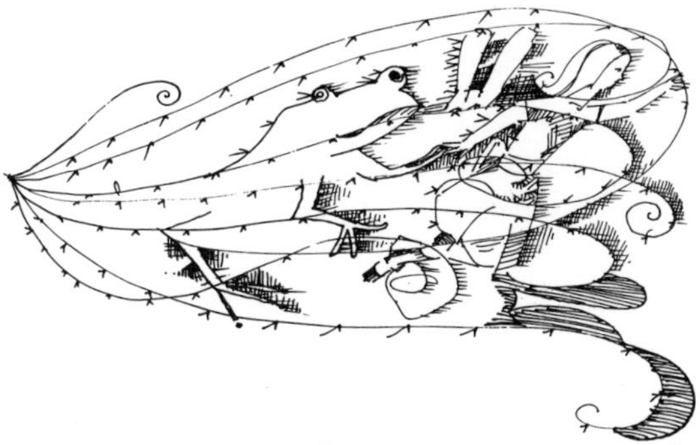

'Oh!, Wait Awhile,' the monotonous voice
Was a fear that they furtively shared,
While a thousand small clinging fingers
Had them rudely and painfully ensnared.
And they had no suitable clothing on,
And their minds were quite unprepared.

'It's disgraceful and hardly fair,' they cried,
'To trap us in this cowardly way
When we haven't brought our sandwiches,
Or fed the cat today.
And a scratched and captive audience
Certainly won't want to hear you play.'

The Wait Awhile Vine, quite desperate by now,
Wouldn't loosen its barbed-wire grip.
Who would hear his soporific song,
If he let them give him the slip?
He belled his cantos and quelled his quavers
And their eyelids began to drip.

'Look here, now!' snapped a fine furling figure—
A Walking-stick Palm in full stride.
'Release them at once or I'll rap your knuckles
And slap your nasty fingers besides.
You're giving the forest a bad reputation.
I will not tolerate it!' he cried.

He slapped about in a frightful fury,
His curls flying quite awry.
The Wait Awhile Vine slunk away defeated.
'Bravo, Palm!' you could hear them cry.
The White Rabbit brushed his ears in the mirror—
And Alice's shoes flew by.

The Noisy Pitta finished with a silvery trill and clapped his wings together to suggest applause. The company understood and applauded loudly. A smile spread all over his beak. Nothing but rave reviews, he thought modestly.

But the Echidna was getting rather prickly. No one had noticed him and he was well known as a leading poet in the forest. They should have asked him first, he thought rather indignantly. He stood up and tapped his spoon against his cup very loudly for attention.

'I'll admit the Wait Awhile adventure was mildly interesting,' he said, 'but the Great Fight was a much wider and deeper kind of affair, if you know what I mean.' He looked around the table for approval.

'I was there on the day of the Great Fight,' said the Echidna rather slyly. 'I saw everything. I immortalised it in verse. I'll read you my poem,' he said, suddenly shy and waiting to be persuaded.

'Oh yes, do,' said Alice, knowing the ways of spiky Echidnas. 'We would love to hear it.' So, gulping a quick mouthful of tea for confidence and to oil his voice, he stood up, pushed a curious fern out of his ear, and announced the title: "The Day of the Ding Dong Fight".

He paused and waited for the White Rabbit to stop slurping his tea and when there was absolute silence he continued. In a splendid dramatic voice, putting in all the screams and cries and sound effects, he read his poem.

THE DAY OF THE DING DONG FIGHT

A nightmarish screech tore the forest apart.
Sort of 'Help!' and 'Meeooow!' and all that!
The White Rabbit and Alice rushed to the scene
Where a python was swallowing the Cat.

'Do not eat Cheshire Cat,' Alice cried in dismay,
As they pulled on each tail with their might.
He finally emerged with a terrible 'pop!'
And they all fell about in a fright.

With a slithering, rustling, hungry-like creep
The python slid off to his lair.
The Cat, feigning nonchalance, examined his paws—
He had hardly lost even a hair.

'We have saved you from snake stomach land,'
smirked the Rabbit,
'When you'd just about grinned your last grin.
A python was *almost* excessively fat,
Who had previously been very thin.'

'We have dragged you,' he boasted, 'from death's
very jaws.
You had hardly a tail left to tell.
And yet you've not thanked us properly at all.
Are you rude or not feeling quite well?'

'Why, you bleached big-eared bunyip,'
the Cheshire Cat cried,
As a Green Ring-tailed Possum could vouch,
'You'd give indigestion to old crocodiles.
Bag your head in a kangaroo's pouch!'

These were terms that could only be described
as quite low.
The White Rabbit felt highly affronted.
It was too much to bear from a wild, grinning cat
Whose legs and whose manners were stunted!

There followed a fight of a ding-donging din,
In an immensely uncivilised fashion.
Fur flying, seeing stars, in a whirlwind of fury
They fought with uncharitable passion.

With bellicose roars and pugnacious attacks,
'Till death do us part' was their vow.
Until Alice, who was shocked to the ends of
her bow,
Cried: 'Please stop all this rampage, *right now!*'

They kissed and made up with extremely bad grace,
Because Alice insisted they must.
The fighting was over—no one sure who had won,
But peace had returned, we all trust.

The Echidna said, 'The end,' very nicely and with a degree of determination. He then appeared to bow twice although it was actually hard to tell exactly what he was doing. He looked more like an out-of-work concertina folding up.

The White Rabbit felt his ears go pink. Had he really been that pompous and aggressive? The Cheshire Cat, grateful he had the table to hide under, had the grace to look a little sheepish—if a cat can be said to look like a sheep.

However, the guilty feeling didn't last long. It was difficult for a cat, and particularly a Cheshire Cat, to be caught in such a humiliating position as halfway down a python's throat.

As for being grateful to a Rabbit—that was, as anyone in their right mind would understand, too much for any cat to bear, he thought. And so, he justified his bad behaviour, as naughty cats have an unfortunate tendency to do.

Alice leaned back with a self-righteous smile. Her behaviour at least had been perfect which, she thought with all modesty, was exactly how she always behaved. 'What a lovely poem,' she said to the Echidna. If you were at school I'm sure you'd get a purple certificate.' The Echidna blushed to the tip of each spike and sat down to a murmur of applause. He drank three more cups of tea in rapid succession.

'On due consideration,' said Alice, just as the Echidna was congratulating himself, 'your poem is perhaps a little fierce—almost, one might say, disturbing. Couldn't you write a happier verse?'

'Oh, I always had a flair for the epic poem,' said the Echidna, making a deprecating gesture. 'All the ingredients were there: the largest snake in Australia, the Scrub Python. Why he must have been fifteen metres long!' Alice looked at him severely. She set strict limits on exaggeration.

Beyond that limit lurked vulgarity.

'Well, ten metres, anyway, and that's a fact,' said the Echidna, who was a bit awed by Alice, but who saw no value whatsoever in spoiling a good story.

'What was I saying?' he continued. 'Yes, the largest snake and the maddest cat and the fiercest rabbit. There's Epic material for you. You must agree.'

And they all agreed quickly in case he decided to recite it again.

'And do you have a contribution to make?' The Echidna made a whirling theatrical wave toward the startled White Rabbit, who looked at him in blank astonishment.

'I mean a song or a poem,' explained the Echidna in a superior manner.

'What sort of a poem?' said the White Rabbit in a muffled chocolatey voice, playing for time.

'I mean a poem you wrote yourself. A creative poem,' he added very grandly.

The White Rabbit almost choked on his last mouthful. 'No, I don't,' he said grumpily. 'But, if you'd like to wait, I'll make one up right now.'

'Don't bother,' said the Echidna in a lordly fashion. 'I think perhaps two poets at a picnic are enough.'

At that, the Dragon, who had arrived halfway through the Echidna's poem and had thought of making a poetic offering himself, hurriedly sat down and ate another slice of chocolate cake instead. Alice, at that stage, was inclined to agree and so she started to clear the table.

Just then, there was a scurrying, scuttling noise and through the clearing burst a whole army of beetles, ants, spiders and small frogs. They were all very busy hurrying off to somewhere and Alice was very curious to know where.

Suddenly, there was a loud flapping sound and

overhead a great cloud of birds of all shapes and sizes went swiftly flying by—off to that same mysterious somewhere. Alice was getting curious and 'curiouser'.

'Well, we have to go now,' the Echidna said hurriedly, looking at the fleeing creatures. But he couldn't resist making a speech. 'Thank you for your enchanting tea party,' he said, giving one of his funny folded-up bows. 'And now, farewell.' He waved a flamboyant paw.

'Just a minute,' said Alice firmly. 'Please, tell me first what exactly is going on?' The Echidna, who could always be persuaded to tell or sing a story, stopped and told Alice where everyone was going and why.

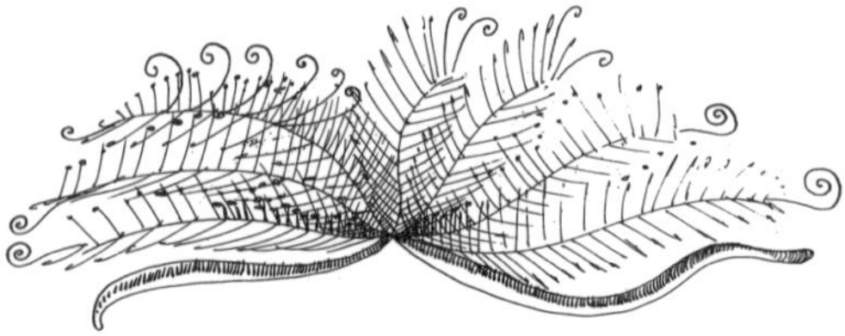

THE NIGHT OF THE LYREBIRD

'It's the Night of the Lyrebird and tonight
  is the time,
The most wonderful night of the year!
Every creature alive in the Rainforest now,
Will fly, hop or crawl to be there.

'It's the night of our concert, our ceremony,
  our song.
Nothing could keep us detained.
You'd have to have measles, sore toes
  or the mumps,
To stay home,' the Echidna explained.

'And now, do forgive me, I'll just join this possum,
An old friend of mine, on the way.
We want to be early, there's a long way to go
And the best seats will be gone if we stay.'

And with that the Echidna waddled off as fast as his little legs would take him and joined a Coppery

Brushtail Possum who was waiting impatiently.

'Wait a minute,' gasped Alice, running after him with the White Rabbit close behind. 'Could we come too?'

'Have you got an invitation?' the Possum asked, stopping and examining them closely with big poppy eyes.

'Yes,' said the White Rabbit, producing a large envelope with what could only be a gold printed invitation inside.

'Oh, well,' said the Possum, impressed with the envelope, in that case I can see no reason why you shouldn't come.'

'Oh, good!' Alice clapped her hands and tried to dismiss the thought that the White Rabbit's very handy invitation might not stand up to close inspection.

They followed a polite distance behind the Echidna and the Possum, taking care not to intrude on, or even listen to, their earnest conversation.

Soon they were swept along on the tide of creatures rushing through the forest. The air was full of sliding and marching, flapping and crunching, hopping and slithering as everyone hurried to get there early and get a good spot.

Alice held on to the White Rabbit with one hand and her hair bow with the other and they whirled along at a brisk pace.

At last, they came to a river and wondered how they would ever get across. Then they saw a group of large crocodiles, each with its tail in the next one's mouth, and they had formed a bridge, a most inspired bridge, right across the river.

'Goodness me!' said the White Rabbit, shaking with fear at the very sight. 'Surely we don't have to cross the river that way. I don't think that would be at all safe.'

Alice had exactly the same uneasy feeling, which

was considerably increased when she saw the late sun glinting on the biggest, sharpest teeth she had ever had the misfortune to see.

'Don't worry,' called the Echidna, skipping across the crocodile bridge. 'There's a national truce in the forest on the Night of the Lyrebird. Perfect harmony must reign in the forest. No one is allowed to even tread on an ant.'

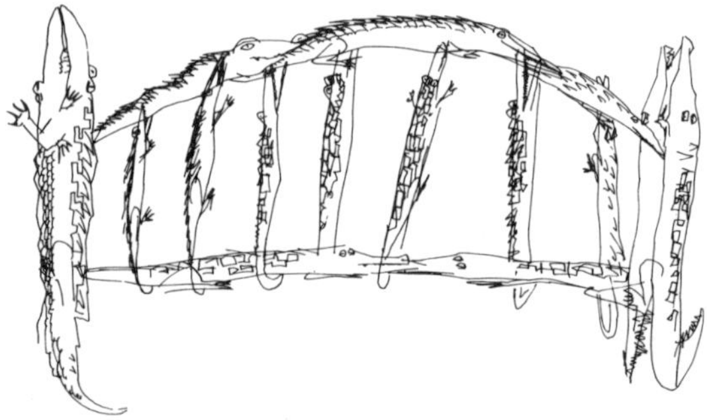

The White Rabbit almost closed his eyes, leaving only a little squinthole, and stepped gingerly on the back of the first crocodile. He felt a wave of fear shiver through him. He stretched out a paw for Alice. She took a deep breath and stepped on the crocodile, too.

Then they ran as fast as they could over the crocodile bridge to the other side. It was terrifying and they both felt extremely brave once they were safely across. The Echidna and the Possum laughed and laughed until crocodile tears ran down their cheeks.

Soon they came to a huge clearing and a splendid sight greeted them. It was like a great cathedral. Tall trees sprang up almost as far as the eye could see and met at the top, creating a living vault. The walls of the cathedral were made of cascading vines and ferns and at the front were two great silvery curtains of Strangler Figs.

Great shafts of light came streaming down through the green dimness and the high branches were festooned with snakes and pythons who hung and dripped over each branch.

The Cheshire Cat, who had been following at a safe distance, took one look at the 'snake trees' and promptly vanished.

On the lower branches perched rows and rows of birds. There were thousands of them. They looked like great chains of brilliant feathered jewels.

The Golden Whistler, the rich blue Azure Kingfisher, the dazzling Crimson Rosella, the scarlet and green Double-eyed Fig Parrot, The Yellow-eyed Tawny Frogmouth, the handsome Noisy Pitta and the Purple-crowned Pigeon, among many others. 'Don't they look beautiful!' exclaimed Alice to the White Rabbit.

On the next rows of branches sat all the moths and butterflies with their luminous wings shimmering slightly.

The whole wide clearing seemed enveloped in living rainbows. It was as if this was the place where rainbows were born, which was not altogether a strange occupation for a great magical rainforest.

On the lowest branches crowded the tree frogs and toads, the possums and the bats, and on the ground large birds and small insects all pushed each other to find a comfortable spot.

Alice and the White Rabbit found a rock that was high enough to give them a view and bare except for a few geckos and a bowerbird.

They waited in the late afternoon sun while every space on every tree filled up and the ground around became extremely crowded.

Suddenly, there was a fanfare of trills and the frenzied chattering and chirping that had been almost deafening quietened down and soon it was so hushed you could have heard a leaf falling.

The fanfare sounded again and from behind the curtain of Strangler Figs the procession emerged and started its slow march around the clearing.

A hundred Noisy Pittas stepped out, all calling their clear trumpet-like sound in the evening air. Their fanfare called to any late-coming creatures to hurry and be ready for the Lyrebird. Behind them marched a hundred Red-eyed Tree Frogs. Their huge yellow vocal sacs were blown up like big drums and they beat out an inspiring drumming rhythm as they proceeded.

Next came a flight of brilliantly patterned butterflies in perfect formation. Their vivid colours and fluttering wings were like a procession of medieval banners blowing in the breeze.

Then a formation of red-headed Brush Turkeys marched past, their powerful legs stamping loudly in time to the drumming. After them came a group of large Emu-like flightless Cassowarys, their blue necks held proudly up and their wild eyes swivelling round. They lifted their feet high in time to the march and then stomped them down.

Stamp, bang, whistle!, they marched as colourful as any troubadors or clowns, while baby possums tumbled in front of them, somersaulting and juggling and waving their bushy tails. Some clever ones even walked on their hands upside down. And hundreds of shining little green frogs leap-frogged past.

Oh, it is a grand procession, thought Alice. I'm sure I will never see anything as wonderful as this again. And she was probably right.

'Back in your places,' thundered a regal, stomping Brush Turkey to the curious chattering youngsters who had crept into the clearing, way beyond the boundaries. They scuttled obediently back to their right places.

Suddenly, in the late afternoon, the Lyrebird walked into the clearing and silence descended.

There was a gasp of wonder as he spread his splendid tail in display. The great feathers on either side curved into the shape of a huge lyre. The famous musician of the forest had arrived! He was their greatest star. A cheer sounded and echoed through the highest trees.

Three times he walked around the clearing like some prince of the forest and the creatures could barely contain their excitement. He imperiously danced and swayed up to his mound in the centre of the clearing and proudly lifting his head called out in the sweetest, clearest voice that he was ready to start his song.

A shiver of excitement rippled through the assembled creatures. Even the trees bent closer to catch each note of the beautiful voice.

Shafts of light came down through the green gloom and he was bathed in a golden light. Then he began his song.

THE SONG OF THE FOREST

Long long ago when the world was born all the
creatures wept with joy.
Clear green and pure were their tears.
Their thanks rained down through the centuries.
They wept for millions of years.

And from their tears the tall trees grew.
They wept a forest of ferns.
And a green misty light came alive in this world.
The Rainforest glow now burns.

A meeting was held all over the planet
Of the creatures who loved their new world.
'The Rainforest will be our cathedral,' they said,
'Where the green banner of life is unfurled.'

We will never stop raining our tears of joy.
We will celebrate life for all time.
No one will forget our future dream
While the Rainforest stays our shrine.

And all life teemed and birds lived songs
And butterflies carried the light.
We promise to guard our forest of life
All of us here tonight!
All of us here tonight!

And solemnly, all the tiny voices took up the song and sang it with the Lyrebird. And as they sang, slowly night filled up the forest and all the stars came out and darted their glittering light down through the trees and some of them came closer and hung on the trees for the creatures to see.

Thousands of voices could be heard now singing "The Song of the Forest" and the music rose up to the vaulted canopy and filled all the forest. Alice and the White Rabbit thought they would burst with excitement.

And then all the creatures stepped out and slowly walked around the clearing, each carrying a tiny star of light and singing their song. As the soft paws or claws or thin birds' legs carried them round, they each made a swelling in the great bursting song until it resounded and shook the very forest and beat around their heads like wings.

Then the Lyrebird, still singing, walked slowly off his platform and disappeared into the darkness of the forest. The eyes of the creatures followed him. Then one by one they vanished quietly into the forest to go home and sleep. The great song gently faded away, slowly and softly, until it remained only in their memory, where it would sing softly to itself until next year.

The stars faded and went back to their high places in the sky and the forest settled into a soft velvety darkness.

Alice and the Rabbit were so tired that they stayed where they were in the clearing. They gathered a pile of dried leaves and, with the Cheshire Cat, curled up, pulled the blanket of leaves over them and went to sleep.

The Echidna stayed near them to guard them from harm, although there was no harm in the forest that night. No bird would even snap at a worm. No creature would forget the song of life on that night. So the Echidna sighed and smiled, lowered his spikes, rolled himself into a ball and he, too, went to sleep.

THE DARK WAY HOME

Next morning when Alice and the White Rabbit awoke, there were hundreds of little creatures tidying up the large forest clearing, straightening up the ferns, brushing the trees, plumping up the downtrodden moss and plants and putting everything back in its place.

The Echidna stretched and wiggled his spikes. 'It was a great concert, wasn't it?' he asked happily.

'Oh, yes,' agreed Alice. 'I'll never forget it.'

The Cheshire Cat was not there the next morning. As usual he had vanished, but Alice wasn't concerned. She was used to him popping in and out of her life. He frequented timeless cat paths known only to Cheshire Cats. He was probably at home this very minute.

Alice and the White Rabbit and the Echidna lay in the morning sun watching everyone clean up and feeling very lazy.

Three of the cleaning possums found flutes and whistles left over from the concert and they struck up a merry song to encourage the others to work.

Alice and the White Rabbit jumped up and started skipping and dancing together around the clearing. It was such fun, and soon the others followed them and Alice taught the baby possums how to skip. Soon everyone was skipping around the forest clearing and not much work was done.

It got very hot and damp and soon they all collapsed under a tree to rest.

'How long do you think we've been here—in the Rainforest, I mean?' Alice asked the White Rabbit.

'Oh, ages,' he yawned. 'Days or months. I'm not sure.'

'My goodness!' Alice cried. 'I had no idea it was that long. Everyone at home will be dreadfully worried. We really must go home now before something else happens.'

'Should we?' said the White Rabbit lazily.

'I never thought about it before,' said Alice rather worriedly, 'but, how do we get home?'

'Well, how did we get here?' asked the White Rabbit logically.

'Down the long rabbit hole,' Alice answered promptly.

'Well, what comes down must go up,' said the White Rabbit firmly, but not quite so logically.

'I don't really know if that will work,' said Alice, 'and besides, I don't remember where the rabbit hole is. Do you?'

'No. Not that particular one,' the White Rabbit admitted sadly.

'Oh, dear!' Alice cried. 'It might take us years to find it and then we might not be able to fall upwards.'

'Well. How did you get home from Wonderland?' The White Rabbit was being sensible again.

'I just woke up and there I was,' said Alice.

'Well, let's go to sleep and see if we can wake up at home,' they both cried together.

They curled up under the tree and after a great deal of concentrating, and warmed by the sun, they fell asleep.

Much later, they woke up to a fragrant perfume. The forest creatures had left a pile of fruits beside them for their lunch.

Bananas and pineapples, mangoes and pawpaws, it was a delicious surprise and soon they were munching contentedly. The Echidna and several small possums and birds joined them. It turned into a delightful picnic.

'Dear, oh, dear!' Alice cried suddenly, halfway through a banana. 'Look where we are. We are still here. We went to sleep and we didn't wake up where we thought we would. We are still where we are.'

Even the Echidna had difficulty working that out. The others didn't even try.

'I gather you want to go home,' said the Echidna sadly.

'Yes,' said Alice. 'It's not that I want to leave. I just don't want everyone at home to get worried. Can you tell us how we can get there?'

'Well, I don't want you to go home,' said the Echidna slowly. 'But I would if I could, but I don't know.'

Alice smiled sympathetically. She knew exactly what he meant and she admired his sentiments.

'I know. I know,' said a small possum, jumping

up and down excitedly with the enormity of his idea. It was the first one he had ever had.

'Tell us!' they all cried.

'The Guardian's gatekeeper, the Tawny Frogmouth,' the small possum cried quite innocently. 'You could ask him. He's absolutely famous for telling people the way to things.'

'I'm quite sure he is,' said Alice, a trifle unkindly. 'Goodness knows where you might end up if you followed his directions. Probably in the Antarctic or on the moon.'

'That might be interesting,' mused the White Rabbit.

'But I do appreciate your idea,' said Alice, noticing the small possum's crestfallen face. 'It was very thoughtful of you and if you haven't actually encountered the Tawny Frogmouth, you could have no possible notion of how confusing he can be.'

And with that, the possum cheered up immediately.

'There must be someone who could tell us the way home,' said Alice. 'I know the Guardian could, but I don't think he'll speak again for years and years and I really can't wait that long. We have to think of someone else.'

They all sat there and thought very hard, and then they walked around for a while and thought some more. It was fairly exhausting and they had to sit down again.

While they sat and thought, an idea was starting to form in Alice's mind. 'I think the younger trees that grow near the Guardian would know,' she said. 'They are like his pupils. He has taught them dream collecting. They must know how to get home. Yes, I think they might.'

And she jumped up with excitement. 'Let's go now and ask them.'

'We'll come too,' said the others.

So they set off and, leaving the scene of the great concert, progressed through the forest. Soon they came to the river but there was no crocodile bridge there now to help them across.

Now, there was only the deep river flowing and some decidedly sinister-looking shapes lurking in the water that might well be the fierce remains of the bridge.

There was no truce in the forest now and Alice felt that it would be wise to view crocodiles with the deepest suspicion.

They wandered along the river bank looking for a way across when they came upon a small boat wedged up in the sand.

'The very thing we need!' cried the White Rabbit. 'Now we can sail across.'

'We can't just take someone's boat,' said Alice sadly. 'That would be dreadfully rude.'

'Well, we could just row over,' said the White Rabbit, 'and then we could row it back and return it.'

'And then we'd be right back where we started,' Alice cried in desperation.

'And that's the best place to be, I always say,' enthused the Echidna.

'And at least we would have been to the other side,' the White Rabbit added convincingly.

Just then the Noisy Pitta flew up. He had heard Alice was leaving and had come to say goodbye.

'There's a rope on the front of the boat,' said the Noisy Pitta when he had heard the problem. 'When you get to the other side I'll get all my brothers and cousins to tow it back.'

Alice was delighted and jumped up and down. 'You are so clever,' she told the Pitta.

And so, Alice and her friends climbed into the boat and, singing a happy river travelling song, they sailed across the water until finally they came to the other side.

Then down flew all the brightly coloured birds and, taking the rope in their beaks, towed the empty boat back to the other side. The boat bounced in the small waves like a fairy toy and the birds spread out their wings like banners.

As Alice was now too big to ride on the Echidna's back, they all trudged slowly along through the Rainforest, pushing back the ferns, seeing all the wonderful sights and reluctantly coming closer to the place of the Guardian.

When they reached the Tawny Frogmouth's tree and saw him sleeping there like a gargoyle on a cathedral, they tried to creep past without waking him but he heard them rustling past in the ferns and cried, 'Stop!'

'You mustn't disturb the Guardian,' he warned.

'No. We have no intention of disturbing him,' Alice said very earnestly, and boldly kept walking on with the creatures following behind.

The Tawny Frogmouth believed Alice, so he offered to give her directions. 'I have a poem that

explains everything,' he said generously.

'Thank you very much indeed,' said Alice, 'but I remember the way.' She hurried off.

They came at last to the clearing where the Guardian loomed gigantically over the dark pool.

Alice and all the creatures looked up at him with awe. 'I can't believe I actually spoke to him,' whispered Alice.

The tall young trees on the other side of the pool were watching her and Alice addressed them with respect.

'I have come to ask your help,' she said. 'I wonder if you can tell me the way home.'

An excited wind swept among their branches and the dark water of the pool rippled uneasily. The creatures moved backwards but Alice stepped forward.

'Look into the pool,' the trees made their soft sighing sound and sent the shadows of their leaves rippling and weaving over the pool. When the surface cleared there was an image of Alice and the White Rabbit asleep on a sunny bank near her home.

'Oh, look!' cried Alice, and the creatures, forgetting their fear, all rushed forward and looked in the pool.

'How do I get there?' begged Alice, turning to the trees. 'Please tell me.'

'You must jump into the dark pool,' they sighed.

Alice and her friends drew back in fear. The water looked icy and terribly deep.

But the golden image of sleeping Alice remained floating on the centre of the pool, and Alice knew that she must have the courage to make the leap.

She turned bravely and said goodbye and thank you to her friends who waved sadly back at her. Then she turned to the Guardian and said very softly: 'Can I come back one day and see how my dream has grown?'

A nodding grew among the Guardian's branches and the trees on the opposite side all sighed, 'You will remember. You will remember.'

Waving one last time, she grabbed the White Rabbit's paw and ran with him and leaped right into the middle of the pool and right into the middle of her image.

They did not feel the icy water they expected but seemed to enter a soft, spinning cloud that whirled them through coloured mists of time. Looking up they could see the anxious faces of the rainforest creatures watching them in a high circle far above. They spun faster and faster and the faces of their friends grew distant and vanished.

Colour and light spun around them and became a golden colour, like the sun on a long summer's afternoon. They blinked against the light and opened their eyes, and they were at home on the grassy bank and the Rainforest was on the other side of the world.

But it was also in another place. A place no maps would show. It was in the mind of a little girl called Alice and she would never forget.